The Adventures of

Goliath and the Burglar

Other ADVENTURES OF GOLIATH
that you will enjoy reading:

Goliath's Christmas

Teacher's Pet

The Adventures of Goliath

Goliath and the Burglar

Terrance Dicks
Illustrated by
Valerie Littlewood

SCHOLASTIC INC.
New York Toronto London Auckland Sydney

ISBN 0-590-47617-3

Text copyright © 1984 by Terrance Dicks. Illustrations copyright © 1984 by Valerie Littlewood. All rights reserved. Published by Scholastic Inc., 730 Broadway, New York, NY 10003, by arrangement with Barron's Educational Series, Inc.

12 11 10 9 8 7 6 5 4 3 2 1   3 4 5 6 7 8/9

Printed in the U.S.A.   40

First Scholastic printing, November 1993

CONTENTS

The Adventures of Goliath

Goliath and the Burglar

Chapter One

The Puppy Nobody Wanted

David had always wanted a dog. Always, always, always.

When he was a baby, his mom and dad had asked what he wanted for Christmas, and David had said, "Doggy!"

His mom and dad had laughed and bought him a big toy dog. That kept him happy for a while—but only a little while.

As David got bigger, he made it very clear that all he really wanted in the world was a real live dog.

As a matter of fact, although David grew a little bigger every year, he never really grew *very* big.

He was usually the smallest or second smallest in his class, and he was always in the front row for class photographs.

David was an only child, and sometimes it felt a bit lonely.

But if David was small, he was *very* determined.

Every birthday and every Christmas when they asked what he wanted, it was always the same answer.

Not a bike or a video game or a camera or a fishing rod. Not even a hamster or a gerbil or a turtle or a kitten. David wanted a dog.

But his mom and dad always said their apartment was too small. "If we ever get a house of our own, with a garden . . ." Then, one day, they moved.

It wasn't a house, but it was a much bigger apartment, half a house really. It was actually in the same street, so David didn't have to change his school or lose his friends. Most important of all, it was a ground floor apartment, the bottom half of the house—and it had a garden.

The minute he saw the garden David said, "*Now* can I have a dog?"

"It's only a very small garden," said his dad doubtfully.

"That's all right," said David quickly. "I only want a very small dog."

It took a lot more arguing and persuading, but in the end his mom said, "Well . . . he has wanted a dog for ages. And it would be company for him."

And his dad said, "Well, as long as it really is a small one."

David said joyfully, "It's Saturday tomorrow. Can we go to the pet shop?"

So they did.

David loved the pet shop. He often went there on his way home from school. There were puppies and kittens and rabbits in big cages in the

window. There was a parrot on a
stand near the door who squawked,
"Ullo!" when you came in, and "Bye,
bye!" as you left. There was a big
cage running along one wall with
what seemed like hundreds of tiny
tropical birds. There were lots more
cages filled with hamsters and
gerbils and white mice.

There was a more than usually mixed bunch of puppies in the shop when they arrived. Some Labrador puppies, fat and sleek and shiny like baby seals. Some baby sheep dogs having pretend fights and jumping all over each other. There were even a couple of dumpy little Bulldog puppies. All the puppies were leaping and growling and barking, till the inside of the cage was a whirl of fur.

They went inside the shop and talked to the lady in charge. That's when the problems started.

All the dogs in the shop were pedigree-dogs, purebreds, the kind that win prizes. They were all very expensive, and what was worse, they were the kind of dog that grows very big.

Things didn't look very promising.

Suddenly, David spotted a ragged

bundle of white fur in the corner of the cage. "What about that one?"

"Oh, you don't want him," said the lady. "I bought some mongrel puppies cheap from a lady who wanted to get rid of them. The others were all nice lively little things, and they all went quickly. That one's such a sad little thing, nobody wanted him."

As they watched, the scruffy little puppy crept out of the corner over to the big feeding dish, which still held a few scraps of dog food.

Just as he reached it, a fat Labrador pup shoved him casually out of the way, wolfed up the scraps, and went back to play.

Sadly the little dog went back to his corner.

"I'll have that one," said David. "Please!"

"You don't want him," said the pet shop lady again. "He's the runt, smallest and weakest of the litter." She lowered her voice. "Sometimes they don't live very long."

"I want *him,*" repeated David firmly. "Please!"

And no one could talk him out of it.

Finally David's dad gave in and

bought the little puppy. It didn't cost very much—which was just as well, since they now had to buy a collar and a leash and a basket and a feeding bowl and a water bowl.

David cradled the shivering puppy in his arms, his parents picked up the rest of the gear, and they set off home.

When they arrived, David settled the puppy in its basket in front of the fire.

"What are you going to call it?" asked his dad.

"What about Scrap?" suggested his mother. "Or Midge?"

"His name is Goliath," announced David, and everybody laughed.

David had read the Bible story of how David the shepherd boy had defeated the giant Goliath with his slingshot, and the name stuck in David's mind. The names David and Goliath seemed to make a natural pair. If Goliath wasn't exactly a giant, at least he could have a giant's name. "Perhaps he'll grow to fit it," thought David. And to everyone's astonishment, that's exactly what happened!

Chapter Two

The Growing of Goliath

It all happened amazingly quickly.

Dogs aren't like people, you see. It takes a human being eighteen or twenty years to reach full size.

Dogs grow up in six months.

Goliath just grew and grew and grew.

The way David looked after him had a lot to do with it.

At first, Goliath just sat shivering in his basket, too frightened to come out, too fed up to eat.

David had to coax him with warm milk and little scraps of tasty food.

He cuddled him and stroked him and hugged him. He took him for walks around the little garden.

When Goliath was old enough, David made sure he was taken to the vet for his shots. "More expense," grumbled David's dad. Puppies have to be inoculated against dog diseases. Since Goliath was so weak to start with, David wasn't taking any chances.

"Bit of a runt," said the vet, as he examined Goliath. "Seems to be coming along all right though."

And Goliath was.

David made his parents try all the brands of dog food on the market, till they found one Goliath liked.

It was called, "Wuffo, Builder of Champions."

Maybe it had a magic ingredient
or something.

Goliath started to grow.

He changed from a timid,
shivering, tiny puppy to a great big
bouncy, noisy puppy.

He bounded about the apartment,
knocking things over and chewing
things up.

He chewed up David's dad's best
leather slippers. He chewed up

David's old toy dog, pretending to
fight it. He even chewed up his own
dog basket, gnawing down all the
sides till there was just a round circle
on the floor. They didn't bother
buying him a new basket. By then
Goliath was getting too big for
baskets anyway.

At night, he liked to sleep on
David's bed.

That was fine when Goliath was

still tiny. David liked having the
little warm bundle curled up at
the bottom of the bed.

But Goliath kept on growing—and growing and growing. Before long he needed most of the bed for himself. It was David who had to curl up at the bottom.

Some mornings David woke up and found himself on the floor. Goliath had pushed him right out of bed.

Eventually, David's mom fished an old mattress from the spare room and laid it on the floor beside David's bed, and Goliath slept on that.

At least David could get some sleep at night. Goliath liked having his own bed.

But that didn't solve all the other problems.

Goliath needed exercise, lots and lots of it.

David had to take him for long walks every morning before school, and every afternoon after school.

Not to mention a final walk just before bedtime.

By the time he was six months old—Goliath was *enormous*.

He looked like a mixture of all the biggest dogs you've ever seen. Part German shepherd, part St. Bernard, part Irish wolfhound, part Mastiff. David's dad said he was part elephant as well.

Since boys grow so much slower than dogs, David wasn't very much bigger.

In fact, Goliath was bigger than he was.

Somehow passers-by couldn't help smiling as they saw them go by, the very small boy being tugged along by the enormous dog. "Who's taking who for a walk then?" people used to ask.

David didn't mind.

He had his dog at last, and he was
blissfully happy. David and Goliath
adored each other.

Every morning Goliath woke
David up in time for school by
licking his face.

He howled sadly every morning
when David had to leave the house to
go to school.

Every afternoon, Goliath welcomed him home with great, booming barks.

That was weekdays of course.

Saturdays and Sundays, Goliath nudged David out of bed so they could go downstairs, have their breakfasts— one bowl of cornflakes and one bowl of Wuffo—and go off to the park for their morning walk.

Goliath loved Saturdays and Sundays.

He loved television as well. When they came back from their Saturday morning walk, Goliath would plonk himself down in front of the television and bark for it to be turned on. He was very fond of cartoons.

David taught Goliath to "speak," to bark for treats. They had special games, too, like "bears" under the rug.

Suddenly, David was the envy of all his friends.

People were always coming around asking if they could take Goliath for a walk with David.

David's parents still grumbled a bit of course. David's dad said you couldn't move in the apartment without stumbling over that great hairy lump of a dog.

David's mom said that most of her housekeeping money went on dog biscuits and cans of Wuffo.

But really they both loved Goliath just as much as David did. In fact, everyone loved Goliath.

Or nearly everyone.

There was just one exception—and unfortunately it was a very important one. Mrs. Richards—their landlady.

She didn't care for Goliath at all.

And that's where the trouble started.

Chapter Three

Goliath Must Go!

The whole house belonged to Mrs. Richards.

She lived in the top half. David and his parents—and Goliath—lived in the bottom half.

Mrs. Richards didn't like dogs.

She wasn't too pleased when they got Goliath in the first place. She told David's dad that she'd never said they could have a dog. In fact it was against the rental agreement.

David's dad said he was very

sorry, he hadn't realized.

If Goliath had stayed a small dog, or even an ordinary-sized dog, they might have got away with it.

Perhaps Mrs. Richards would eventually have forgotten he was there.

But you couldn't forget about Goliath.

Not when he crashed about the house, sounding, as Mrs. Richards said, more like a donkey than a dog.

Not when he gave tremendous barks that shook the window panes and rattled pots and pans on the shelves. And above all, not when Goliath was so affectionate. He had a gentle, trusting nature, and believed that the whole world was his friend. When David took him for a walk in the park, Goliath would rush up to strangers, wagging his tail. When

they got over the shock and realized
he was harmless, most people gave
him a pat or stroked him. Sometimes
children would give him candy.

   David tried to discourage this,
because candy is bad for dogs.
Goliath encouraged it as much as he
could. He loved candy, especially
chocolate.

Goliath naturally thought Mrs.
Richards loved him just like
everyone else.

Since she lived in the same house,
he treated her as one of the family.

When Goliath was especially fond
of people, he liked to give them a
kiss.

This meant putting his paws on
their shoulders and delivering a wet
and sloppy lick on the face.

Not everybody liked it.

Mrs. Richards hated it.

The first time Goliath did it, she
screamed and rushed back upstairs
to wash her face.

After that, whenever she saw him
she shouted, "Shoo!" and "Get off!"
and waved her umbrella at him.

Goliath thought she was playing.

Once he snatched the umbrella
from her and ran away with it. David

had to chase him all around the house to get it back.

All this was bad enough.

But what really finished things was the tea party. Every Friday afternoon, Mrs. Richards entertained some of her lady friends.

She served them tea and cakes and cookies on plates with paper doilies on them. Then all the ladies sat around and chatted about what a terrible state the world was in, and how badly young people behaved these days, and so on.

One day, when one of these parties was going on, Goliath padded silently upstairs.

Mrs. Richards's living room door was ajar. Goliath pushed it open with his nose.

He ambled in, looked into the room, and saw Mrs. Richards and two

other ladies staring at him.
(Although Goliath didn't realize it,
they were frozen with horror.)

Goliath noticed that one of the
ladies was holding a chocolate
cookie in mid-air.

Naturally Goliath thought it was
for him. He "spoke," giving a great
booming bark. Having done his
trick, Goliath ambled over to her,
took the cookie from her fingers, and
wolfed it down.

The old lady gasped.

Looking around, Goliath saw a
whole plate of chocolate cookies on a
little table nearby.

It only took him a minute or two to
finish the whole plateful. Licking the
plate nice and clean, he gave a
couple of woofs of thanks and trotted
back downstairs.

As soon as her friends had gone,

Mrs. Richards came tearing down to see David's parents.

"I've put up with a lot from that horrible animal," she said, "but this is too much! Either it goes or you go! I'll give you till Monday to make up your mind!"

With that she stormed off upstairs.

David looked appealingly at his parents. "You wouldn't, would you?" he pleaded. "Not get rid of Goliath?"

There was an awkward silence.

Then David's mom said, "Of course, we hate the idea as much as you do. Goliath is a bit of a nuisance sometimes, but we've grown very fond of him. But if Mrs. Richards insists . . ."

"She can't just turn us out, can she?" asked David.

"Well, there is a no-pets rule in the agreement we signed," said David's father. "She could make things very difficult if she took us to court."

Goliath was sitting in the middle of the room, looking from one to the other. Somehow he seemed to know he was being talked about.

David ran up and hugged him. "I

don't care," he said. "Let her throw us out then. I'd sooner live any old place than lose Goliath."

"Now be sensible," said his father gently. "You know how lucky we were to get a bigger apartment in the same street. We've got to have somewhere to live, you know, somewhere we can afford, somewhere near your school and my job. If it really does come to a choice between Goliath and this apartment . . ."

He didn't finish the sentence, but David knew all too well what he meant.

Goliath would have to go.

Chapter Four

David to the Rescue

David didn't get much sleep that night.

He lay in his bed wide awake for most of the night, hugging Goliath, as if someone was going to try and snatch him away right now.

It wasn't really as bad as that, of course. Tomorrow was Saturday, so they had the whole weekend to think about it.

David's mom and dad had done their best to console him. "We'd make sure he went to a very good home," said his mom.

His dad said, "Maybe if we're very nice to Mrs. Richards and apologize for all the fuss she'll change her mind."

David didn't believe it. Mrs. Richards wasn't the sort of person to change her mind. Not about Goliath, anyway.

Next morning, as usual, his parents went out to do the weekend shopping at the big supermarket in the center of town. David, as usual, stayed home with Goliath.

Usually they watched Saturday morning television together, but David felt too fed up for TV. He just sat slumped in the armchair, with the set not even turned on, staring at the blank screen, wondering what he was going to do.

Goliath lay at his feet, looking in a puzzled way at the empty screen, wondering when the programs were going to start.

Suddenly David heard a noise.
It sounded a bit like a key in the lock of the front door, and for a moment he thought it was his parents coming back. But the noise

went on longer and was somehow more fiddly than a key, and it ended in a sort of splintering sound.

Someone was forcing open the front door.

They were being burgled!

Now you might think Saturday morning is a very unlikely time for a burglary, but any policeman will tell you it's not. Burglars don't all come at the dead of night.

A lot of them are what the police call "walk-in thieves." They come and break into a house in the morning when people are out shopping, pick up any valuables they can find, and clear off. Sometimes they will rob as many as a dozen houses in a morning. This burglar was one of those. He had seen David's parents go out, and he thought the house must be empty.

The TV was in the living room downstairs, and the front door was in the hall just outside.

David crept to the door and, pushing it nearly closed, peeped through the gap.

He was just in time to see the edge of a metal bar appear in the gap between the front door and the frame, and the lock forced off in a shower of splinters.

The door opened, and a man came into the hall. He wore jeans and an old windbreaker, and his unshaven face looked hard and vicious.

He closed the door behind him, stood listening for a moment, and then crept past the living room door and up the stairs.

Goliath had been sitting listening to the noises from the front door, with his head cocked and his tail

wagging. He liked visitors.

"Big silly thing!" thought David. "Some dogs would bark and growl and chase the burglar off, but not Goliath. He loves everyone—even burglars."

As a matter of fact, in spite of his size Goliath was actually rather on the timid side. He didn't chase cats, cats chased him. Once in the park, Goliath had been attacked by a very small but very fierce Pekinese. Goliath had been terrified and had run for his life. No, he wouldn't get much help from Goliath, decided David. He would have to deal with things himself.

He could hear the burglar moving about in the room over his head. Luckily there was a telephone in the hall.

Moving very quietly, David picked

it up and dialed 911. Almost
immediately a lady's voice said
briskly, "Which service do you
require?"

"Police, please," whispered David.

A moment later a man's voice
came on the line. "Police here, can I
help you?"

"I hope so," said David. "We're
having a burglary." He gave the man
his name and address.

"Anyone else in the house with

you?" asked the man.

"There's our landlady, who lives upstairs."

"Right. You just keep out of the burglar's way. Get out of the house if you can. We'll have a car around in no time."

Carefully David put the phone down, hoping the burglar hadn't heard the little ting it always made.

He stood in the hallway, hesitating. He could get out easily enough, but that would mean leaving Mrs. Richards alone with the burglar.

Somehow that didn't seem right.

He could no longer hear movement upstairs. David realized what had happened. The burglar had gone farther up the stairs—into Mrs. Richards's apartment.

Suddenly David heard a scream

from upstairs, and a gruff voice shouting threats.

David had a sudden inspiration. His coat was hanging up in the hall, and in the pocket there should be half a bar of chocolate.

David grabbed the chocolate from the coat and held it up. "Speak! Goliath, speak!"

At the sight of the chocolate Goliath gave a series of barks that seemed to shake the house.

The noise from upstairs stopped— and was replaced by the sound of feet pounding down the stairs.

David had another inspiration. There was an old rug on the living room floor, and he and Goliath often used it for one of their games. David would get under it and growl, and Goliath would jump on him. They called it playing "Bears."

Goliath wagged his tail as David picked up the rug. But this time David didn't get under it. He just stood there, waiting.

The pounding feet came nearer.

Chapter Five

Goliath's Triumph

As the burglar came rushing down the stairs, David lifted the rug high and threw it over the man's head. "Bears, Goliath! Bears!" shouted David.

Goliath threw himself on the burglar, barking joyfully. Bears was his favorite game. How nice of this man to come around and play with him.

Goliath's charge knocked the burglar off his feet, and he fell with a

crash, arms and legs waving wildly.

The more he fought to get free, the more he got tangled in the rug, and the more he shouted and struggled, the more Goliath joined in the game, barking furiously and jumping on him again and again.

At last the man managed to wriggle free.

With a yell of fear, he threw open the front door and dashed out into the street—straight into the arms of two enormous policemen, who were just getting out of their car.

The policemen grabbed his arms, and the burglar shouted, "All right, all right, I won't give any trouble. Just get that monster of a dog off me. I can't stand dogs!"

Goliath had followed him into the street, still barking. He felt disappointed that the nice man didn't seem to want to play any more.

David hauled off Goliath, one of the policemen hauled off the burglar— just as David's parents came up the street on their way back from the supermarket. David's mom was so amazed, she dropped her shopping bags. Together with one of the policemen they went up to the top of the house. They found Mrs. Richards sitting in the middle of her bedroom floor, frightened and shaken, but not really hurt.

Apparently the burglar had snatched her purse, stolen some jewels, and was trying to frighten her into giving him more money when he heard the barking and turned and ran.

"You had a lucky escape," said the policeman. "All thanks to this boy here, and his dog. It's a good thing for you they were in the house!"

David's mom and dad helped Mrs. Richards to an armchair, and David's mom made her a cup of tea.

The policeman had a cup as well. "Yes, a lucky escape," he repeated as he sipped his tea. "Those fellows can turn very nasty if they don't get what they want. Good thing you had a nice big dog in the house."

"Dog?" said Mrs. Richards dazedly.

The policeman patted Goliath. "It's all thanks to this fellow here—and his owner of course. The boy gave the alarm, and the dog frightened the burglar off *and* caught him for us as well, so you'll even get your money and jewels back."

Mrs. Richards said, "Thank you, David. Thank you." She looked at Goliath. "And thank you, too, Goliath!"

David's mom had produced some cookies with the tea, and Mrs. Richards took one from the plate and handed it to Goliath. He snapped it up, leaned forward, and gave Mrs. Richards a sloppy kiss.

Mrs. Richards actually leaned forward and kissed him back.

Of course, after that, there was no more talk about Goliath going. In fact, Mrs. Richards said he was welcome to come up and have tea with her and her friends any time he liked.

Goliath was the hero of the street.

All David's friends came around to see him and wanted to hear the whole exciting story.

The man from the local paper came around, and David and Goliath had their pictures in the paper. There was even a little article about the attempted robbery, telling how it had been stopped by Goliath, who was described as "a trained

guard dog." The story made it look as
if Goliath had done all the work,
while David just stood by and watched.

David didn't mind. As long as he
could keep Goliath, he was happy to
let his dog take all the credit.

Goliath took it all for granted.

He did notice that people were
making a bit of a fuss over him, but he
didn't mind that.

When the story came out in the
paper lots of people sent him
presents, including a whole crate of
"Wuffo."

Goliath enjoyed all the praise and attention, though he was a bit puzzled by it. After all, why should people make such a fuss over a game of "Bears"?

About the author

After studying at Cambridge, Terrance Dicks became
an advertising copy-writer, then a radio and television
scriptwriter and script editor. His career as a
children's author began with the *Dr Who* series and he
has now written a variety of other books on subjects
ranging from horror to detection.